For my granddaughter Chloe Szukala, who shares her life and love

—S.C.

To Janie, Tony, and Mary Kate

—P.B.

THIS IS A BORZOI BOOK PUBLISHED BY ALFRED A. KNOPF · Text copyright © 2011 by Shutta Crum · Jacket art and interior illustrations copyright © 2011 by Patrice Barton

All rights reserved. Published in the United States by Alfred A. Knopf, an imprint of Random House Children's Books, a division of Random House, Inc., New York.

Knopf, Borzoi Books, and the colophon are registered trademarks of Random House, Inc. · Visit us on the Web! www.randomhouse.com/kids · Educators and librarians,

for a variety of teaching tools, visit us at www.randomhouse.com/teachers · Library of Congress Cataloging-in-Publication Data is available upon request.

ISBN 978-0-375-86711-8 (trade) · ISBN 978-0-375-96711-5 (lib. bdg.) · The text of this book is set in Mrs Eaves. · The illustrations in this book are

pencil sketches created digitally. · MANUFACTURED IN CHINA · June 2011 · 10 9 8 7 6 5 4 3 2 1 · First Edition

MINE!

story by **Shutta Crum**

pictures by **Patrice Barton**

Alfred A. Knopf 🐕 New York

"Mine."

"Mine."

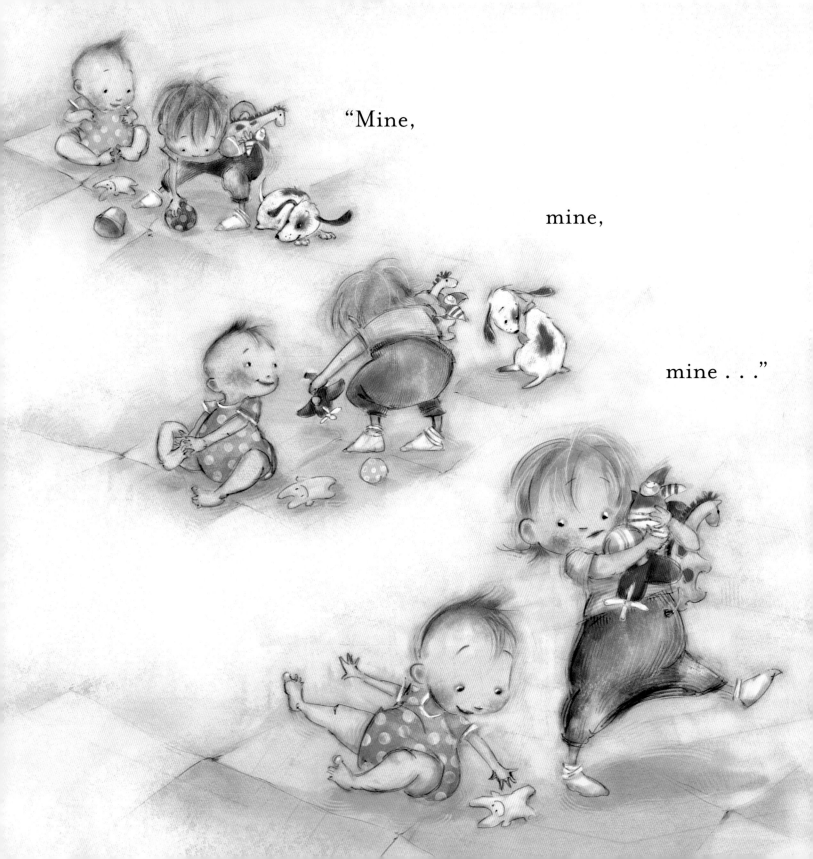

"Mine,

mine,

mine . . ."

"MINE!"

"Mine!"

"Mi—"

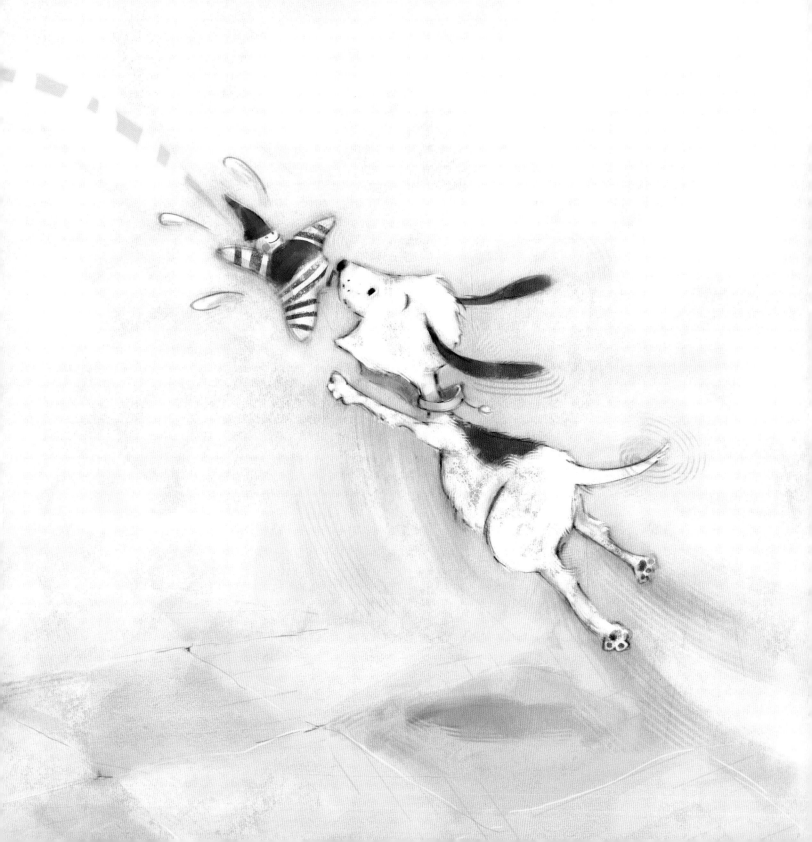

"Woof?"

"Mine!"

"Mine!"